Tadpole Books are published by Jump!, 5357 Penn Avenue South, Minneapolis, MN 55419, www.jumplibrary.com

Copyright ©2023 Jump. International copyright reserved in all countries. No part of this book may be reproduced in any form without written permission from the publisher.

**Editor:** Jenna Gleisner **Designer:** Molly Ballanger **Translator:** Annette Granat

**Photo Credits:** Varina C/Shutterstock, cover; Shutterstock, 1, 8–9 (background); ezhenaphoto/Shutterstock, 2mr, 3; Louis-Paul st-onge Louis/Alamy, 2tr, 4–5; Clover No.7 Photography/Getty, 2br, 6–7; iStock, 2bl, 8–9 (foreground); Viktoriia Likhonosova/Shutterstock, 2tl, 10–11; Katrina Wittkamp/Getty, 2ml, 12–13; StockImageFactory.com/Shutterstock, 14–15; Oleksandr Briagin/Shutterstock, 16tl; pazham/iStock, 16tr; Happy Together/Shutterstock, 16bl; Veres Production/Shutterstock, 16br.

Library of Congress Cataloging-in-Publication Data
Names: Gleisner, Jenna Lee, author.
Title: La hora de dormir / por Jenna Lee Gleisner.
Other titles: Bedtime. Spanish
Description: Minneapolis, MN: Jump!, Inc., 2023.
Series: Las primeras rutinas | Includes index. | Audience: Ages 4–7
Identifiers: LCCN 2021059740 (print)
LCCN 2021059741 (ebook)
ISBN 9798885240208 (hardcover)
ISBN 9798885240215 (paperback)
ISBN 9798885240222 (ebook)
Subjects: LCSH: Sleeping customs—Juvenile literature. | Bedtime—Juvenile literature.
Classification: LCC GT3000.3 .G5418 2023 (print) | LCC GT3000.3 (ebook) | DDC 392.3—dc23
LC record available at https://lccn.loc.gov/2021059740
LC ebook record available at https://lccn.loc.gov/2021059741

LAS PRIMERAS RUTINAS

# LA HORA DE DORMIR

por Jenna Lee Gleisner

## TABLA DE CONTENIDO

**Palabras a saber** . . . . . . . . . . . . . . . . . . . . . . . . . 2

**La hora de dormir** . . . . . . . . . . . . . . . . . . . . . . . . 3

**¡Repasemos!** . . . . . . . . . . . . . . . . . . . . . . . . . . . . . 16

**Índice** . . . . . . . . . . . . . . . . . . . . . . . . . . . . . . . . . . . 16

# PALABRAS A SABER

cepillo

lavo

leemos

limpio

peino

pijama

# LA HORA DE DORMIR

**Yo limpio.**

**Me lavo el cuerpo.**

Me lavo el cabello.

Me pongo la pijama.

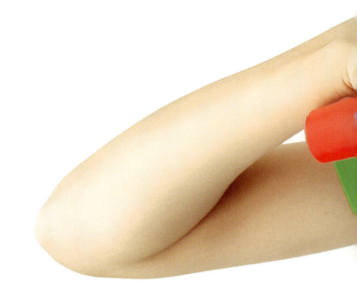

cepillo de dientes

**Me cepillo los dientes.**

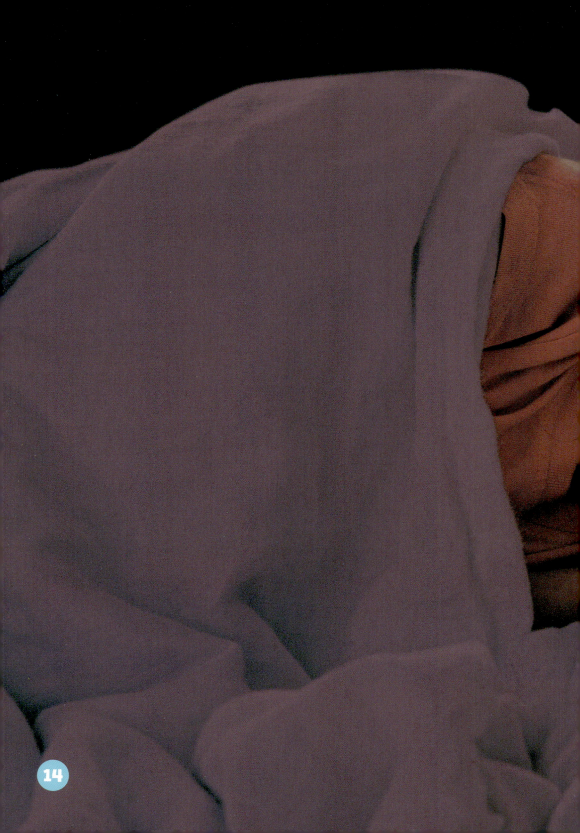

¡Buenas noches!

# ¡REPASEMOS!

¿Cuál acción de abajo no forma parte de la rutina de la hora de dormir en el libro?

# ÍNDICE

**cabello** 5, 9
**cepillo** 11
**cuerpo** 4
**dientes** 11

**lavo** 4, 5
**leemos** 13
**peino** 9
**pijama** 7